Dara's Cambodian
New Year

by Sothea Chiemruom

Illustrated by
Dam Nang Pin

HALF MOON BOOKS
Published by Simon & Schuster
New York London Toronto Sydney Tokyo Singapore

HALF MOON BOOKS
Simon & Schuster Building, Rockefeller Center, 1230 Avenue of the Americas, New York, NY 10020. Copyright © 1992
by The Children's Museum, Boston. First HALF MOON BOOKS edition 1994. Originally published by Modern Curriculum
Press as part of the Multicultural Celebrations Series created under the auspices of The Children's Museum, Boston. Leslie
Swartz, Director of Teacher Services, organized and directed this project with funding from The Hitachi Foundation. All
rights reserved including the right of reproduction in whole or in part in any form. Designed by Gary Fujiwara. Photographs:
2, The Children's Museum, Boston; 6, Leonard Stuttman; 16, The Children's Museum, Boston; 18, Susan McCartney.
HALF MOON BOOKS is a trademark of Simon & Schuster. Manufactured in Mexico. 10 9 8 7 6 5 4 3 2 1
ISBN: 0-671-88607-X

"Lokyay says that Lokta is sad. She is worried
about him."

I could only hear little bits of the conversation
between my mother and Aunt Sophola as I came in
the door from school. They were talking about
Grandmother and Grandfather.

1

"Well, this is only our second New Year in the United States. Now that it is April, and *chaul chnam thmey*, entering the New Year, Lokta is homesick for Cambodia. He longs for the days of peace there. He is sad because we were forced to leave our homeland," Aunt Sophola said.

"I know how Lokta feels," my mother answered. "I like to remember the times when we were happy there, too. But it is good that we escaped the war and terrible times in Cambodia."

"Yes, we all miss Cambodia, but not as badly as Lokta. He just sits in his room and feels sad. We are all trying to make a new beginning in the United States."

I thought about how much easier it had been for me to get used to the United States. The food, the language, and my school did not seem strange to me anymore. But it was different for my grandparents.

"Well, it is April 13, New Year's Eve," my mother said. "We will do our best to celebrate as we did in Cambodia. Maybe that will cheer up Lokta. Aunt Sophola, remember how we cleaned the house to welcome the *New Angel*? We all had new clothes—and streamers and flowers were hung everywhere. It was a wonderful three days of celebrating with family and friends!"

I looked down at the picture in my hand—the painting that had won me first place in the school art competition. I could remember every word the principal had said when he called me up to the front of the auditorium.

"Dara, you have only been in our school for a short time, and you have had to learn many things about the United States. With your paintings, you are helping us learn about your beautiful country. We all thank you for that and hope to learn more."

I was so proud. I wanted to share how I felt with Grandfather and everyone in my family. But now that I know how sad Grandfather is, I must wait until a better time. I will wait until the New Year has passed. I put the painting back into my folder and went into the living room.

"Why, Dara, you're home already?" asked my mother, surprised. "Then you can help Aunt Sophola and me in the kitchen. We have to prepare the food to take to the temple tomorrow morning."

"Where are Lokyay and Lokta?" I asked.

"Your grandmother is in the kitchen and your grandfather is in his room," Aunt Sophola said. "Your grandmother thinks he is just a little sad about the coming New Year. But that is nothing for you to worry about. How was school?"

As Mother, Aunt Sophola, and Lokyay cooked, I had a snack. The food filled my stomach and thoughts filled my head—thoughts of what I could remember about our beautiful Cambodia. I knew why Lokta is sad. He remembers the times of war and the times of peace. He misses his homeland.

Slowly an idea came to me—a way to make *chaul chnam thmey* a very happy one for Grandfather and our whole family. But it would take a little work.

I got up very early the next morning and went to my grandfather's room. As usual, he was having his morning tea.

"*Sur sdey chnam thmey,* Lokta," I said, greeting him for the New Year.

"*Sur sdey chnam thmey,* Dara," he said to me. "It is early. I am surprised to see you."

"I'm up early to work on special New Year's gifts for the family, Grandfather, but I need your help to finish them."

I spread out my paints and papers.

14

"I want to give each person one of my New Year's paintings. I have done these sketches, but I want to make sure the details are right before I paint them."

Lokta picked up one of the sketches.

"Why, this is a picture of our house in Cambodia decorated for New Year's Eve," he said, surprised. "But to make the picture right, Dara, you must paint an altar. It must have five candles, five incense holders, a bowl of perfumed water to wash the *Buddha*, and fruit and flowers. And don't forget the *bay sey*, the rolled banana leaves."

I worked on the painting as Lokta picked up another sketch.

"This is our temple where we learned *Buddha's* teachings and prayed with the monks," Lokta said. "But here you must add the sand mountain. It is important because we hope we have as much good health and happiness as there are grains of sand."

Then he picked up the last two pictures. "These are good, Dara. You have shown the children playing *teanh proat* just right. The clothing is correct too, but make sure the girl is wearing a brightly decorated *hol.*"

"What do you think of this one, Grandfather?" I asked as I showed him the painting that had won the award. For a minute he was quiet and I was afraid he didn't like it. At last his face broke into a very broad smile.

"This one is very, very special. I have never seen the
countryside of Cambodia look more beautiful. It is
just as I remember it . . . it is just as I want to
remember it."

"It's as you can always remember it, Grandfather.
This picture is for you," I said proudly. "May the
New Year bring you health and happiness."

Lokta looked up, put his hand in mine and said,
"Come, let us share your beautiful pictures with the
rest of the family. After all, it is the beginning of the
New Year."

Glossary

bay sey (BUY SAY) banana leaves rolled in finger shapes

Buddha (BOOD-uh) an Asian religious leader who founded the religion of Buddhism, the main religion of Cambodia

chaul chnam thmey (CHOOL chah'NAHM tah'MAY) a phrase that means "entering the New Year;" it is the Cambodian name for New Year

Dara (dah-RAH) boy's name

hol (HOHL) cloth that is wrapped to make a skirt or other clothing

Lokta (lock-DAH) Khmer (or Cambodian) for grandfather

Lokyay (lock-YAY) Khmer (or Cambodian) for grandmother

New Angel (NOO AHN-jel) the guardian and protector for the New Year

Sophola (soh-PAHL-ah) aunt's name

sur sdey chnam thmey (SOO-ur sah'DAY chah'NAHM tah'MAY) Khmer (or Cambodian) greeting meaning "Happy New Year"

teanh proat (DIEN PROHT) a Cambodian tug-of-war game

22

About the Author

Sothea Chiemruom grew up in Phnom Penh, Cambodia. Since coming to the United States with his family in 1981, he has attended high school and college. He is involved with many Cambodian youth organizations in the Boston, Massachusetts area.

About the Illustrator

Dam Nang Pin was born in Siemréab, Cambodia. He grew up in the capital city of Phnom Penh, where he attended the University of Fine Arts. After spending a year in a refugee camp in Kaôh Kong, Cambodia, he was allowed to come to the United States in June, 1990. He left his mother and sister in Cambodia. Dam Nang enjoys using watercolors, as well as creating large oil paintings. He plans to continue his art studies at the Museum School of Fine Arts in Boston, Massachusetts.